This book belongs to:

_____

_____

_____

First published 2013 by Walker Books Ltd
87 Vauxhall Walk, London SE11 5HJ

This edition published 2014

2 4 6 8 10 9 7 5 3 1

© 2013 Lucy Cousins
Lucy Cousins font © 2013 Lucy Cousins

The author/illustrator has asserted her moral rights

Illustrated in the style of Lucy Cousins by King Rollo Films Ltd

Maisy™. Maisy is a registered trademark of Walker Books Ltd, London

Printed in China

British Library Cataloguing in Publication Data:
a catalogue record for this book is
available from the British Library.

ISBN 978-1-4063-5229-0

www.walker.co.uk

Maisy Learns to Swim

Lucy Cousins

WALKER BOOKS
AND SUBSIDIARIES
LONDON · BOSTON · SYDNEY · AUCKLAND

Maisy is going swimming today. Time to get ready!

Have you got everything you need, Maisy?

Eddie and Tallulah are coming too.

Eddie is already wearing his goggles. "I'm an underwater diver!" he says.

Maisy and Tallulah get ready together in the changing room – it's so busy!

Nice swimsuit, Tallulah!

The pool looks very big.
Maisy dips her toes in.
Ooh, it's freeeezing!

Maisy and Tallulah get
into the pool slowly.

The water goes swish-swash, splish-splash. It feels nice!

Their swim
teacher is
called **Poppy**.
She's a really
good swimmer.

"Let's try and warm up,"
Poppy says. "Wiggle your
toes and lift your arms
in the air!"

Next, everyone holds on to their floats and kicks their feet.

Now it's time to try floating!

Maisy pushes her belly up to the ceiling and stretches her arms out like a starfish.

Poppy shows everyone how to blow bubbles. Tallulah takes a deep breath ...

puts her nose in the water ...

and blows out really hard –

blup-blup-blup!

Maisy wants to try too.

1-2-3 . . .

bubbly ubbley ubble!

Look at all the bubbles!

"Well done everyone!" says Poppy
"That was a great lesson.
Up the steps we go!"

Maisy feels shivery out of the water, so she wraps herself up in a fluffy towel. Aaaah, that's better!

Now she needs a nice, warm shower.

"Do you like swimming, Maisy?" asks Tallulah. "I think it's much more fun than bath time!"

"Me too," says Maisy. "Floating is my favourite!"

Now it's time for a snack. Yummy! "When is our next lesson?" says Maisy. She can't wait to go swimming again!